DO'S AND DONUTS

RAISED AND GLAZED COZY MYSTERIES,
BOOK 30

EMMA AINSLEY

SUMMER PRESCOTT BOOKS PUBLISHING

CHAPTER ONE

"I don't think I understand how all of this works," Brett Mission said from the front seat of his pickup truck. It was a rare day off for the sheriff of Dogwood Mountain County.

"She's a wedding planner, Brett," Maggie Sharpe, his devoted fiancé, informed him. "We're three weeks away from the wedding, sweetheart. And everything is falling apart."

"I know things have been stressful, but I've told you all along that I don't care if it's in the middle of a cornfield in jeans and t-shirts. All I care about is marrying you. I wish we'd done it already."

"I know, I know," Maggie said calmly. "But you and I both know that there are a lot of people who care about us and want to be there, too. Your girls, Bradley and Wyatt, just to name our children alone."

"I should have married you the second we graduated high school," Brett said. He leaned over the center console of his truck and twirled a piece of her hair around his finger as he spoke. "I wish I had been less of a knucklehead and not wasted over two decades of my life without you."

Maggie smiled and shook her head. "That's not so easily said when you think about the girls and my son," she said. "We might not be the same people if that had happened. Trust me, I regret many wasted years without you by my side, but I also think we had lives before now that made us into who we are."

"I know. I just hate seeing you so stressed out about what's going to be the happiest day of my life." He frowned. "It doesn't seem fair."

"That's why I hired a wedding planner," she said. "Her name is Vicky Byrd, and she comes highly recommended."

"Highly recommended by the nineteen-year-old you just hired to help out at the donut shop," Brett reminded her.

"She might be Haley's cousin, but Vicky is middle aged, not a teenager." Maggie felt a shiver of concern despite her words. "When I spoke with her, she seemed very capable. She was eager to start. She's only been in this area a few months and is hopeful she can eventually set up a business for herself here."

"Where is she from?" Brett asked.

"She just moved back to the area from Dallas." Maggie sighed. "I did run a background check on her before I gave her all of the money I had for the wedding, sweetheart."

Brett smiled. "I know you ran a check on her. Brooks already told me you had him do it." As the chief of police in their home town of Dogwood Mountain, Missouri, Brooks Macklin was Maggie's go-to when she had a concern she was not keen on filling Brett in on. "I just wondered where she had come from before, now that she wants to build up clientele for her business."

"From what I understand, she worked for a large bakery in the Dallas-Fort Worth area," Maggie explained. "She moved back here to be closer to family and wants to build up her business here, which is good for us because she gave me a steep discount."

"You gave her a lot of money," Brett said. "That was with a discount?"

"Keep in mind some of that money is to pay the rest of what we owe on the wedding cake and the caterer," Maggie said. "We had deposits down already, and she will just pay the balance, so we don't have to worry about it."

Brett sat back up in his seat. "That's worth it, I suppose," he said. "How did Ruby take the news that you had hired a caterer at the last minute?"

"Honestly? I think she was relieved, but she insisted that we still use the old barn at her place where Myra and Brooks tied the knot."

"If you're overwhelmed right now, so is she," Brett said. Ruby Cobb worked alongside Maggie as her business partner and best friend. She had a busy life outside of the donut shop as a former executive chef, who penned cookbooks in her spare time. She also owned a small farm and was on the city council. The extra stress from the donut shop sometimes pulled her away from her other projects, never mind adding catering a wedding to her long list of things to be responsible for.

"The catering company costs a lot of money because they are also setting up the venue," Maggie explained. "Chairs, tables, the decor, all of it."

"So, all you and I have to do is show up and get dressed," Brett said. "I'm starting to see the point of hiring this woman."

Maggie leaned over the console and planted a loud kiss on his cheek. "I love it when you come around to my way of thinking." Brett grinned and reached for her. He started to tickle her sides when his phone began to ring.

"No," Brett groaned as he sat back in his seat. "It's my day off. What are they going to do without me for an entire week when we're on our honeymoon?"

Maggie chuckled to herself and stared out the window while he answered the phone. Her mind turned to her own work woes. Since the first of the year, Orson Hawley had suffered a stroke and retired. She'd hired young Haley Byrd to help out around the main location in Dogwood Mountain. Her son Bradley's donut shop in Hunter Springs had endured one appliance breakdown after another through the month of March and part way into April. Both hot water heaters had given out within days of each other. The furnace for the entire building was next, followed by a major plumbing leak that led to the place closing for three full days while a team descended on the place to fix it. In less than a month, she had burned through the maintenance fund she had for both locations for the entire year. The Cake My Day Bakery had opened around the first of the year, and the Hunter Springs Donut Shop had already lost a number of staff members to it. Maggie sent her own staff over to help out as much as possible until Bradley could hire and then train new people, but the strain was getting to all of them.

"I have to go," Brett announced when he hung up the phone. "I'm so sorry."

"It's okay, Sheriff." Maggie smiled. "It's not like I don't know what I'm getting into by marrying you."

Brett nodded as he turned the key and started the truck. Maggie gazed over the lake once more before he pulled out of their favorite parking spot and headed back toward the road into town.

"So much for time away from the office."

"Is everything okay?"

"Not really, but it will be," he said. "We just had two staff members walk off of the job in the middle of their shifts at the jail."

"That sounds like a big deal," Maggie said. "What are you going to do?"

"Well, for starters, I'm going into the office to interview five new employees and to check on the progress of the three we've had in training to see if they are ready to step up just yet," Brett said.

"Whoa, that sounds like a lot," she said. "I'm sorry I asked."

Brett laughed as he pulled away from the lake road and hit the two-lane county road that led back to

Dogwood Mountain. Maggie's phone rang as they passed by the second lake entrance. "Your turn." Brett grinned as she answered the phone.

"It's Ruby," Maggie said when she glanced at the screen. "Hello?"

"Maggie, where are you?" Ruby asked her breathlessly.

"Just leaving the lake," Maggie said. "What's the matter?"

Ruby sighed into the phone. "It's the deep fryer," she said. "I stopped by to check on inventory for tomorrow and I found the entire kitchen covered in oil. The fryer must have leaked overnight and now we have our very own oil slick."

"Oh, you're kidding," Maggie said. She closed her eyes and pinched the bridge of her nose.

"I only wish I was," Ruby said. "I need help."

Maggie ended the phone call with a promise to show up right after she went home and changed into grubby clothes.

"What's wrong now?" Brett asked her.

"The deep fryer leaked all over the kitchen."

Brett gasped. "Oh no. What are you going to do?"

"I have absolutely no idea," Maggie said with a nervous laugh.

CHAPTER TWO

"Cat litter," Naomi Gardner said from the back door of the donut shop an hour later. She stood in the doorway with a large bag of the stuff in her arms.

"Cat litter?" Maggie questioned. She stood in the middle of the oil-covered floor with a mop in one hand and the other hand holding on desperately to the edge of the sink. Her pants were covered in oil. Her hair was soaked in it as well, after falling in it three times.

"Yes, cat litter," Naomi said. She set the large bag on the ground in front of her feet and produced a razor knife from her back pocket. She slid the knife across the top of the bag. "I just bought out the supply of cat litter at the store. I have ten more bags in the back of my car. Myra and Brooks are headed to Hunter Springs for more."

"That's absolutely brilliant." Ruby beamed from the other side of the kitchen. She clutched the edge of the baking table. "I wish I had thought of that myself. Go on and just turn that bag over right there and we'll come for the rest of them."

Naomi smiled and dumped the bag over in front of the door. Ruby slowly began her way around the table and headed for the automatic donut machine. Not one square inch of the kitchen had been spared from the oil. Maggie worried about the cooler and the storage room as well, but so far, she had not been able to check on either.

Ruby made her way toward the door. She grabbed a broom on her way and began spreading the mound of cat litter out when she was close enough.

"I bought new brooms," Naomi said when Ruby went to work on the cat litter.

"Might as well save those to replace these ruined ones," Ruby told her. "When this is all said and done, I think we'll end up having to replace most of the cleaning supplies that we've been using."

"So, what happens now?" Myra Sawyer Macklin asked from the swinging door between the kitchen and the dining area. She held a bag of litter in her hands. "We brought these from the county animal shelter instead of driving all the way into Hunter Springs. I left them a sizable donation for their help."

"That was brilliant," Maggie said. The smell of fryer oil filled her head leaving her nauseous and irritable, so she forced herself into hopeful cheerfulness.

"Thanks," Brooks said behind his wife. "I have ten more bags here. Do you want me to just start opening them up and pouring them out over the floor?"

"That's exactly what we need to do," Ruby said. Her hair stuck up all over the back of her head. Like Maggie, she had taken more than one spill in the slick mess. "We should start on either side of the room and work our way toward the middle."

"Then what?" Naomi asked.

"Then we call in a cleaning crew to clean it all up," Maggie said, shaking her head. "And we all enjoy an unexpected day off from work."

Maggie followed the cat litter path toward the front of the donut shop. She wiped her feet carefully on the large rug Myra had dragged over from the front door. She'd carried her phone with her and arranged for the clean-up crew to come and remove the litter the following day once the rest of the oil was absorbed. For a few hundred dollars more, the company promised to leave the donut shop sparkling clean. Maggie agreed to pay for the extra service, figuring it would be worth it.

"Everything is set," she announced when she returned to the kitchen. "We just have to make sure the litter is spread over all of the oil before we leave, and they will see to everything else."

"Seriously?" Naomi paused in the process of opening up another litter bag and stared at her. "We don't have to come back and clean this up?"

Maggie shook her head slowly. "We just have to return the day after tomorrow to a clean donut shop," she said. "You guys go on and enjoy the day off and Naomi, can you please let everyone else know we're closing? I'm going to hang out with Bradley for a little while tomorrow morning, and then stop by and check in with Vicky."

"Is something going on?" Ruby asked. She had previously expressed concern over Maggie's wedding planner.

"No, I just couldn't reach her cell phone the last time I tried," Maggie said.

"That's not good," Myra said.

"She lives in the dead zone in Hunter Springs," Maggie said. "She doesn't always have cell service, so I'm going to stop in and check with her."

Another hour passed before the remaining floor was covered with cat litter and everyone was ready to leave. Maggie walked out of the back door last, and Myra and Brooks headed out the front. Maggie drove the small distance back to her home. As soon as she was there, she sat down at her kitchen table to take a breather. She folded her hands under her chin and gazed at the calendar on her wall. Three weeks and three days. The wedding was so close she could almost taste the wedding cake.

She picked up her phone and dialed Vicky's phone number. The phone rang twice before a new recording picked up. "The wireless customer you are trying to reach is no longer available." Maggie hung up and immediately dialed her again. The recording played a second time.

Maggie decided to try another method. She brought up her email and fired off a fast message to the address Vicky had given her. The email bounced right back from the server. She set the phone on the table and shuddered slightly. Myra's words came back to her. This was not good. She stood up and sent a quick text to Brett. A visit to the wedding planner would not wait until she was finished helping out at the Hunter Springs location the following day.

Brett responded with a phone call as she headed

out the door toward her car. "What's going on?" he asked right away.

"Vicky's cell phone now says she isn't available," Maggie said. "I have a sinking feeling about this."

"Okay, but like you told me the other day, she lives in a dead zone," Brett said. "It could be that her phone didn't even pick up the call."

"That's what I hope, but I emailed her as well, and the email came back right away."

"Oh, no," Brett said. "Let me know what you find out. I have to get back to my office for the next interview."

Maggie hung up her phone and set it on the passenger seat. She backed out of her driveway and headed straight toward the highway. She had to watch her speed because she felt the urge to push down on the accelerator and speed toward the answer to her questions about the state of her wedding.

CHAPTER THREE

Maggie drove up to the small bungalow with white and yellow trim and parked her car in front of the single car garage. She checked her own cell phone for service as she headed for the front porch. Maybe the area wasn't the dead zone she thought it was. Her phone display showed two bars of signal.

The day was a bit overcast and chilly, much like her current mood. Maggie ascended the stairs and glanced through the front windows at the darkened living room. The curtains that had hung in the windows were gone. She closed her eyes and forced herself to calm down as she approached the door. Curtains had to be washed sometimes. She deliberately kept her eyes averted from peering into the room again. She wanted to give the woman the chance to appear at the front door and explain herself before she jumped to any conclusions about where she had gone and what she had done with the money she'd been paid.

When there was no answer to her first knock, Maggie balled up her fist and knocked as firmly as she could without injuring her hand. She waited and counted to thirty before she exhaled slowly. No answer. Enough time had passed that she was sure Vicky was not home.

Maggie cupped her hands around her eyes and looked through the living room window again. She waited for her eyes to focus and stepped back when it was clear that the furniture that had been in the room was gone. The very couch she had sat down on less than a week before and written out the check to the woman had apparently vanished into thin air. She moved slowly to the window on the opposite side of the porch and looked inside. She could see through the empty dining room and into the small kitchen.

Any sign of life had disappeared. Maggie let go of a string of words that would have made Orson proud. Anger pounded in her head. She turned away from the porch and quickly descended the steps. She decided to walk around the side of the house and see what she could see inside the small bedroom Vicky had used as a home office. As she expected, the room was vacant.

She pulled her phone out and immediately called Ruby. She wanted to call Brett first, but she knew he was likely in the middle of another interview. They all had their crises, it seemed. "Ruby?"

"Hey, Maggie," Ruby answered. "I'm having a difficult time hearing you."

"Yeah, I'm at the wedding planner's house," Maggie said. "I only have a couple of bars on my phone."

"Is everything alright?" Ruby asked.

"No, it's not," Maggie said. "She's gone."

"She's what?"

"Gone. Out of here. Vanished," Maggie said. She turned back toward the front of the house. "There was no answer at the front door. I looked through the living room window and all her furniture is gone. Same with the dining room, kitchen, and her office."

"Oh, Maggie. I am so sorry."

"Yeah, so am I," Maggie said. "I should have known this was too good to be true. She seemed so eager to help me out."

Ruby groaned. "Yeah, and that was a red flag for me, but I sure don't like that it seems I was right about her."

"I know. You tried to tell me it was too easy," Maggie admitted. "I guess I'll head to the donut shop and see how things are going with Bradley."

"Are you sure she left nothing behind? Maybe she's in the process of moving and you still have a chance to recoup some of your money from her."

Maggie stood outside of her car with the driver's side door open. "There are another couple of windows on the right side of the house that I haven't looked in, but she just moved to town. It doesn't make sense that she'd be moving already."

"I know, but you might as well check it out just to be sure."

"Hang on." Maggie shut the car door and walked along the side of the front porch down the small sidewalk that led to the back yard. She looked inside the first window to a bedroom she had not seen before. "There's nothing and the next window is probably a bathroom. It's too high."

"Probably nothing helpful in that window anyway," Ruby said.

"One more window and then I'm at the back of the house," she told Ruby. "I don't want to go into the back yard." She stepped up to the window sill. The bottom of the window was barely eye-level.

"Can you see anything?" Ruby asked.

"Not yet." Maggie grumbled. "The yard goes down a little hill." She stood on her toes and cupped her free hand around her eyes.

"Maggie? You just got quiet," Ruby said a moment later.

"Oh, my gosh." She strained to stand up as high as she could. "Ruby, I can see a pair of legs. On the floor. There is someone on the floor!"

"Are you sure? Can you see into the room well enough to tell if it's a person?"

Maggie looked behind her. She spotted a large, decorative stone near the garage. "Hang on. I'm going to pull this stone over so I can stand on it," she said. She set the phone down and quickly lugged the stone over to the side of the house and dropped it in front of the window. She clung to the side of the house as she stepped up, then picked up her phone again. "Okay, I can see a pair of legs halfway in the room. The person appears to be in the hallway as well."

"Are you sure there is a person and not just a pair of pants?" Ruby asked.

"I'm sure," Maggie said. "I can see a pair of legs. No shoes on the feet. Dark socks."

"You'd better call Brett," Ruby said. "I'll let you go for now. Call me back as soon as you can."

"I will," Maggie said. Immediately afterward, she

dialed Brett. "I'm in Hunter Springs at Vicky Byrd's rental house. There's a body inside."

"Wait, what? You found a body?" Brett asked.

"I can see legs and socks. The house has been emptied of furniture, but there is definitely a body in the back bedroom."

"Maggie, are you sure? Brett asked. "Are you one hundred percent sure?"

"Absolutely sure," she said.

"Go to your car immediately and lock the doors. I'll be there in less than five minutes."

CHAPTER FOUR

Maggie waited until Brett arrived with a slew of his deputies before she backed her car out of the driveway to make room for the coroner's van. She stood back, hugging her arms around her middle while she waited. Brett forced the front door open and headed inside.

Thirty minutes later, Brett emerged from the back of the house and met her at her car where she'd parked it a little way down the road. "We're still processing the scene, but we have a woman inside, deceased," he said.

"Okay," Maggie said. She leaned against her car as she watched Brett head back to the house.

Ten minutes later, Maggie pulled her phone out of her pocket and answered it. Ruby had called back, likely going crazy wondering what was going on. "I'm outside waiting for the coroner to bring the body through," she whispered into the phone. "I'm pretty far away though, so I don't know what I'll be able to see."

"What in the world is going on there? Did you find anything out?"

"Brett is here along with about half a dozen deputies," Maggie said. She spoke slightly louder, but still kept her voice low. "The coroner showed up right after."

"This might be a stupid question, but they have confirmed that the woman is dead?" Ruby said.

"They have confirmed that someone inside that house is dead, but I don't think they have said for sure who," Maggie said.

"Well, maybe not, but it's a little suspicious that the woman renting the house hasn't been heard from in several hours," Ruby replied. "I'm jumping to conclusions, but I think it's a safe guess that Vicky Byrd is the woman lying dead inside that house."

"I don't disagree with you, but until we know, I don't want to assume." Maggie figured Ruby was right and it was Vicky, but she desperately didn't want to believe it, and selfishly didn't want to have to deal with the aftermath if it was.

"I understand that entirely," Ruby said. "To be honest, I really only called to see how you were holding up."

"And how do you think I'm holding up?" Maggie asked.

"I think you're dealing with this the best you can," Ruby said. "You're possibly going to go home and have an emotional meltdown, but right now you're holding it together."

Maggie chuckled and switched the phone to the other ear. She sighed and walked around her car. "I hope I'm holding it together," she said. "This is not what I expected to find here today."

"Probably not, and you're already stressed about so many other things," Ruby said. "I think the best thing you can do is take it one minute at a time. Call me before you leave."

"Sure," Maggie said, stepping away from her car and as close to the house as possible. "I'll give you a call, but it looks like they're coming right now so I'd better go. I want to see if I can find anything out."

"Call me later," Ruby said before she hung up the phone.

Maggie shoved her phone into her back pocket as she watched everything happen around her. Time seemed to stand still as the small crew of technicians in medical garb opened the door to make way for the gurney. Brett reached out a hand to assist the technicians as they lowered it down the small set of steps and onto the ground.

Movement of the gurney stopped, and Maggie watched along as Dr. Marsh, the coroner, slightly pulled the top of the white sheet down. Dr. Marsh said a few words to someone else and nodded toward the body. Maggie scooted even closer and stood on her tiptoes, trying not to appear as morbid as she felt. She knew what she was doing was wrong, but she wasn't sure how long it would take to identify the body, and if it was Vicky, she'd be able to do just that.

Images of Vicky Byrd flashed in her head. She braced herself to see the woman's pale face framed by ringlets of gray and brown hair cut close to her head. Maggie closed her eyes tightly for a brief second and when she opened them again, it took a moment for the face to register before she could process things.

"That's not Vicky Byrd," she gasped. She had no idea who the woman was on the gurney. Instead of Vicky's pale complexion, the woman's skin was very tan, as though she'd spent several years baking in the sun. Her long, dark hair spilled around her head and neck and showed no trace of gray.

"Ma'am?" A deputy she didn't recognize said to

her. "What are you doing here?"

"I umm," Maggie stumbled over her words. "I'm the one who called this in, but that doesn't matter right now. What matters is that the person on the gurney is not Vicky Byrd."

"Is it supposed to be?" the deputy asked.

"What? No, I just…" Maggie hesitated. "Can I talk to Brett, please? This is important."

"Ma'am, the sheriff is rather busy right now. I don't think this is the right time, but you're more than welcome to talk to me and say what you have to say."

Maggie shook her head slowly and took out her phone. She sent a text to Brett telling him it wasn't Vicky.

He looked in her direction and frowned, holding a finger up. Before the deputy could say another word, Brett was at their side.

"I've got this from here, Chris," Brett said. "Go over and see if Dr. Marsh needs anything."

Brett turned to Maggie. "I don't even want to know how you saw her face, but what do you mean it's not Vicky?"

"It's not her. I have no idea who it is, but I've never seen her before in my life." She stood next to Brett while two technicians moved to the white van and opened the back doors while four others lifted the gurney and carefully slid it inside. Maggie jumped when the van doors closed.

Brett waited to speak until the van pulled out of the driveway. "That's the last thing I expected to hear," he said. "We found nothing on the body in terms of identification."

"So, what happens next?"

"Well, next you need to give your statement to one of my deputies," Brett said. He smiled. "It's so close to the wedding I think it would be better if someone else handled that."

"Okay," Maggie said, trying to ignore that the deputy from earlier was probably right and she should have told him what she'd learned instead of bothering Brett. The panic was starting to hit her, and she wasn't thinking straight. "Brett, about the wedding…"

"I just need you to go over what you did and what you saw leading up to calling me about the body," Brett continued. "I'll have someone reach out to Ruby as well since you were on the phone with her at the time."

"But, Brett," Maggie said. "The wedding."

"Don't be surprised if you see Vicky Byrd's photo all over the news right away," Brett added. "For the time being, she is a person of interest in this investigation. That language might become more direct if and when the coroner determines the cause of death is a homicide. We will also be reaching out for any help identifying the dead woman."

"I understand all of that. I'm going to make a statement to your deputy, and I will head over to the donut shop to fill Bradley in on what's going on before the news gets to him and my name is involved," Maggie said. "I realize that the priority right now is the fact that a woman is missing and another one has lost her life, but you need to keep it in the back of your mind that the wedding might have to wait for a little while."

Brett turned his attention directly to her. He took her by the arm and led her back to her car. "Why would you say that?" he said.

"Vicky Byrd is missing," Maggie said, trying her hardest not to act like one of those bridezillas everyone talked about.

"Yes, it appears that she is, but she isn't a close friend or a family member," Brett said patiently. "I don't see why that would have any bearing on the wedding moving forward."

Maggie nodded. "It isn't because she's missing, but what else is missing along with her."

Brett swiped the hat off his head and ran his

fingers through his hair as he spoke. "Then I don't get it," he said. "What on earth could there be to delay the wedding?"

"She has our money," Maggie said. "She disappeared with every last dime of the wedding budget. The check cleared yesterday, and now she's gone. We have no caterer, no wedding cake, no minister, nothing but the venue, and that's just because our generous friend is allowing us to be married in her barn."

"Nothing is going to delay you becoming my wife. I don't care if it's just you and me and our closest friends and our family," he said. "We can serve them peanut butter and jelly and throw paper airplanes at each other. We are getting married, okay? I am not waiting one more day to make you my wife."

Maggie wiped the tears from her eyes and looked up at him again. "You're right. I'm sorry I'm acting this way. I just can't help feeling like this is the worst thing in the world that could have happened and at the worst possible time."

"I love you and everything is going to be fine. I promise," Brett said.

Maggie nodded and urged him to get back to work. She couldn't explain the way she was feeling, but she didn't like it one bit.

CHAPTER FIVE

Maggie drove to the Hunter Springs Donut Shop moments after leaving Brett and the rest of the deputies behind at Vicky Byrd's rental house. She wept openly as she drove the short distance to the donut shop, then stopped to wipe her eyes and catch her breath before she went inside to see her son. She inhaled a deep breath and blew it out slowly before she opened her car door. As she walked, she bit her bottom lip and forced the tears back.

"Hey, Mom," Bradley said as she walked in through the back door of the donut shop. "Fancy seeing you here." He smiled broadly and winked at Zeke Soren, his kitchen manager and dear friend from his time serving in the Navy.

"Morning, Maggie," Zeke said.

"What are you guys up to?" Maggie walked into the middle of the kitchen. "Are those powdered sugar donuts?"

"Not exactly," Bradley said with a knowing grin. He plucked a donut off the platter in front of him and carried it over to her. "See for yourself."

"Do you want me to try it?" Maggie asked.

"Please," Bradley said. He waited while she pinched off a piece of the donut and plopped it into her mouth.

"Whoa," she said and turned the donut over in her hand. "That's not what I expected. What is this?"

"What does it taste like to you?" Bradley asked.

"Well, I taste cinnamon and spices and nuts. Almonds? I think it's almonds," she said. "Almost like those Mexican wedding cookies."

"Yes! That's exactly right." Zeke beamed. "We made Mexican wedding cookie inspired donuts."

"In honor of your upcoming wedding," Bradley added.

Maggie frowned immediately. She turned away from the pair and forced herself to inhale a long draw of air. Tears stung her eyes again.

"What's the matter, Mom?" Bradley asked. He rushed to her side. "What is it?"

Maggie turned back around. She was touched

beyond words by her son's immediate reaction to her distress. "Oh, it's nothing really, in light of everything else that has happened," she said, and ran her finger beneath each eye. "For one, a woman is dead, and another one is missing. The result of that means that the wedding itself is now up in the air."

"What?" Bradley took a step back from her. "What are you talking about?"

Maggie sighed and allowed him to guide her to a stool. She sat down and shook her head. "I hired a woman named Vicky Byrd to plan the wedding," she said. "Everything has been so crazy lately. So, I hired Vicky to handle things from here on out. Anyway, I haven't been able to get in touch with her. Ever since the check I wrote to her cleared, she has been radio silent."

"She was found dead?"

Maggie shook her head. "Not her, another woman in her house," she said. "I went there to see if I could speak with her and find out what was going on. When I got there, I knocked on the front door and looked into the windows, but there was nothing in the house. All her furniture was gone. Everything."

"Where did you find the body?" Zeke asked.

"I called Ruby as I made my way around, looking through the windows on the side of the house as well," Maggie recalled. "When I got to the other side of the house, I spotted a pair of legs in the window. I even dragged a landscape stone over to stand on so I could see better. And they were legs, alright. I hung up from Ruby and called Brett."

"Oh, my gosh," Bradley said. "Did this just happen?"

Maggie nodded. "Just now," she said. "The sheriff's department showed up and the coroner's office after that. I saw the woman's face and I think I expected it to be Vicky, but it wasn't." She shuddered at the memory.

"You have no idea who it was?" Bradley asked.

"It was a woman, and she was younger than Vicky by at least twenty years. Her hair was dark and long. Vicky is an older woman with short, curly hair and very pale skin. I have no idea who she was," she said. The tears flowed again.

"Mom, this is terrible," Bradley said. "I'm so sorry you had to deal with this, but I still don't understand why the wedding is in question. Did Brett decide he needed to postpone it because of the case?"

"No, it's such a minor thing in comparison to the death of this woman and Vicky's disappearance, but when she left, she took all of my wedding money with her," Maggie said. "Like I said, the check cleared.

She cashed it and then at some point, she took off with it. Her rental house is empty, aside from the poor young woman who died there."

"As terrible as it is that this woman took off with your money, that doesn't mean you have to put off the wedding," Bradley said. "I mean, you have an entire crew of people ready and willing to help out, and we have not one but two professional kitchens at our disposal."

"Not to mention that your best friend is a professional chef," Zeke said. "And I'm not a newbie in my own right."

"I know that Zeke, and I appreciate you," Maggie said. She wiped her eyes again. "It's about more than just the money, though. A lot has been going on the past few weeks, and today just adds to that. You have no idea how shallow it feels to say this, but I don't want the wedding to be slapped together, and I really don't want it to take place in the middle of a bunch of other distractions."

"What did Brett say when you told him all of this?" Bradley asked.

Maggie stood up and sighed. "He said there was no waiting," she said. "We are getting married in three weeks, no matter what."

"I have to say I like Brett's perspective on this,"

Bradley said. "I'm not choosing one of you over the other, but in this case, I think Brett is right. Not that it matters what I have to say, but I think postponing the wedding is a big mistake. So, this woman stole your money, as far as we can tell, but you guys are in love, and you belong together. You've waited long enough to be together."

"I think a lot of things have been going on in your life lately, and that feels like a great big burden on you right now," Zeke said. "Of course, you don't feel like it's the right time for a wedding, but the two of us are close enough in age to realize that sometimes, the right time is now. Life is short. Get married and be with the man you love."

"That's really good advice," Bradley said.

Maggie nodded and smiled for the first time in a while. "I think you just hit the nail on the head, Zeke," she said. "Even if I disagree with your conclusion, you're correct about everything being so much to handle right now, and how it all feels like a burden. I do feel like the timing is way off. We shouldn't be getting married right now. We probably should have done it last fall."

"Then why wait at all?" Bradley asked. "If you feel like you should have been married already, that only means that the wedding needs to happen as soon as possible."

"No," Maggie said. "It means the time to act was months ago, but now circumstances have changed. We have to face the fact that our window of opportunity may have already passed."

"I understand you're stressed, but I think you might be overreacting," Bradley said to his mom. He watched her for a moment and simply wrapped his arms around her in a hug only a son could give.

CHAPTER SIX

The next morning, Maggie decided to stop in and check on the progress of the cleaners at the donut shop after the oil leaked from the deep fryer. As she drove to the shop, a thought occurred to her. Haley would be at work the following day. At just nineteen, Haley had applied for the part-time position Maggie had advertised in the local newspaper following Orson's stroke. She was young and friendly, though her work ethic was not on par with Myra's initiative when she started.

It was Haley in the first place who had suggested her cousin Vicky as a last-minute wedding planner. Despite the brief background check she had done on the woman, Maggie trusted in the relationship between her employee and her family member. That was obviously a very big mistake.

She decided it was not something she was going to discuss with the younger woman. Questioning the teen about her much older cousin's whereabouts wasn't something she thought was right. She wasn't sure it was a good idea to do so in general, given the criminal investigation into the woman and the fact that she was weeks away from her wedding with the county sheriff.

Several trucks were parked in the front of the donut shop when Maggie pulled into the parking lot. She drove around the side of the building and into the back alley. She spotted the vacuum truck with a large black hose running from the back of the round tanker into the back door. Maggie could hear the loud hum of the vacuum as soon as she pulled close to the building. She hesitated for a moment, then backed her car down the alley and headed toward her house. It was clear that the work in the donut shop was still ongoing. Maggie didn't want to do anything to interrupt the work or to delay the reopening of the donut shop.

More than ever, she needed to distract herself from the other worries flying around in her head. She pulled her car into the back of her house and parked in front of the garage. She gazed over the addition to the house she had just paid to be completed. Her budget was tight for many reasons, and the house renovation was one of the biggest reasons.

Maggie set her things down and headed straight for the living room. She collapsed onto the couch and covered her head with her arms and laid there for at least an hour. She stared at the ceiling through her folded arms and sighed. She expected the tears to flow again, but nothing came. Not a single tear stung her eyes.

Maggie suddenly felt very small. She was one woman in the middle of her life planning the ceremony to unite herself with the man she loved and wanted to spend her remaining years with. She was a mother, grandmother, and business owner. In a few short years, her life had taken a drastic turn from the direction it was headed. She had come home to Dogwood Mountain, taken on the fledgling business her late aunt had left to her, and made it into a success with a second location and a successful food truck.

She had made a life, and a very good one, but she was just one person. Today, she had found the body of a woman she knew nothing about. Her own worries and concerns seemed silly in comparison, and she was ashamed of herself for worrying about them.

Maggie's thoughts were distracted by the sound of someone pounding on her back door. She sat up and tightened her disheveled ponytail. When she arrived at door, she was surprised to see Ruby standing on the other side of the glass.

"You were supposed to call me this morning," she said when she came inside.

"I'm sorry. I woke up and sat around feeling sorry for myself for a couple of hours. I just drove to the donut shop to get out of the house and came right back home."

"Funny," Ruby said. "I just came from the donut shop."

"Was everything going okay?" Maggie asked.

Ruby followed her into the kitchen and nodded. "Everything is going well. When I went inside, they were meticulously cleaning every last grout line in the kitchen."

"That's why you should be the one in charge," she said. "I never would have thought to check on that. All this stuff just comes so easily to you, meanwhile, I just lie around having a pity party."

"What is going on with you? I don't think I've ever seen you this way," Ruby said.

"A woman is dead, and all I can think about is the money that Vicky disappeared with. I saw this woman lying on the floor of Vicky's empty rental house and I was worried about money. I'm a terrible person."

"I think you need to get out of your funk and get busy figuring out what to do next," Ruby said.

"What do you mean by that?"

"Well," Ruby began. "This isn't the first time you've been faced with unusual circumstances and figured out what to do. Now isn't the time to wallow, it's the time to step into action."

"Maybe I don't have it in me any longer." Maggie sighed and walked around the kitchen table. Before she could say another word, Ruby's phone rang.

"It's Brett," Ruby said before she answered. She put the phone to her ear. "Hello? Here with Maggie. Okay, hold on." She held the phone out for Maggie to take.

"Why didn't you call my phone?" Maggie asked when she answered.

"I tried, but it went to your voicemail," he said. "I called Ruby hoping she might know where you were."

"Sorry," Maggie said. "My phone must still be in my bag. I didn't even hear it ring."

"I just wanted to make sure you were alright, and to let you know a couple of things. One, the coroner has made a preliminary ruling on the victim, and two, we have an identity."

Maggie pressed the speaker button on Ruby's phone and set it down on the table between them. "What happened and who was it?"

"Based on the condition of the victim's body, Dr. Marsh has issued a preliminary ruling of homicide," Brett said.

"She was murdered?" Ruby said.

"It appears that way. When the hair was removed from around her neck, ligature marks were clearly visible," Brett said.

"Who was she?" Ruby asked.

"Her name is Kathleen Lester, owner and operator of the Cake My Day Bakery in Hunter Springs," he said.

CHAPTER SEVEN

The alarm woke Maggie early the following morning. As soon as she rolled over to turn it off, the most awful headache hit her. She rolled back and covered her forehead with her hands. Pressing her palms into her head did nothing to alleviate the pain. She decided to get up and find the bottle of pain reliever she had somewhere in the bathroom medicine cabinet.

Maggie made her way to the kitchen and filled a glass full of water. She took two tablets and chased them down with the water, then turned back to the bedroom to get dressed for the day. She had set her alarm half an hour earlier than normal. After the donut shop was shut down for the day, Maggie planned extra time just to make sure that everything was in place before the day began.

There was another reason she wanted to arrive before the rest of her crew. Nothing had been said so far that led her to think Haley, her newest employee, would not arrive for work as usual. She was scheduled at six, just as the doors opened. Maggie wanted to get busy with her day as fast as she possibly could. Each donut she cut out, every scone she shaped into a triangle or cinnamon roll she assembled was another distraction from the situation she found herself in. The missing wedding planner and the body she had discovered was the last thing Maggie wanted to think about when the cousin of said wedding planner arrived for work. Instead, she planned to be fully immersed in the day's tasks when the girl arrived.

When she walked into the donut shop, the air inside smelled clean. Maggie flipped on the lights as she wandered through the shop. The nice smell permeated the entire space, including the customer restrooms. Maggie moved back to the kitchen and looked more closely around the fryer. She moved the unit away from the wall and looked around behind it. She smiled at the squeaky clean floor between the back of the fryer and the wall. She looked around and under everything and could not see so much as a single speck of litter on the floor.

As a matter of fact, the entire place shone better

than it had in months. Maggie inhaled deeply. Her mood had lightened considerably. She headed for the cooler and began assembling ingredients for her favorite vanilla bean donuts. She filled up her arms and carried the load to the baker's table where she gently set everything down. She then turned her attention to the automatic donut machine. She quickly mixed cake donut batter while the machine heated up and spooned it into the large hopper. As soon as the oil reached the right temperature, the machine would begin dropping donuts.

By the time Ruby turned her key in the back door, Maggie had four trays of donuts on the cooling rack and the first two batches of cinnamon roll dough rising on the table. The rest of the table was covered with trays of cake donuts she had already frosted. She moved around a tray with a shaker of blue and pink sprinkles.

"You're busy this morning," Ruby said when she closed the door behind her.

"I decided to come in early just to make sure everything was ready to go before we started the day," Maggie said.

"Well, you've been quite productive," Ruby said. She plucked a clean apron off of the hook outside of the storage room and tied it around her waist. She frowned when she turned back to Maggie. "Has Haley called in sick today? I got to thinking that she might not come in."

Maggie shook her head. "As far as I know, she is going to be here as usual," she said. "Just so you know, I'm not going to ask her any questions about Vicky. She's just a young girl, and probably has already had to speak with the sheriff's department about all of this."

Ruby nodded. "I agree. She doesn't need to be interrogated while she's at work. To be perfectly honest, though, I'll be shocked if she comes in at all. I halfway expect her to be a no call, no show."

"I had the same thought, and if she doesn't come in, I say let's give her a chance to explain herself," Maggie said. "Of course, if there's no contact, she will be fired, just the same as anyone would be."

"Agreed," Ruby said. She headed into the cooler and returned with a large tub of apples for the apple slaw she planned to prepare for the boxed lunches. "Then we'll be back to square one looking for someone to replace Orson."

"I wonder if he'll be in today," Maggie said.

"He can't stay away." Ruby grinned. "Even if he isn't working any longer, you know he'll never give up his place at the Old Timer's table."

"Thank goodness." Maggie smiled back. She picked up the tray of donuts in front of her and carried them out to the dining room. She carefully slid the tray into the display case and headed back to the kitchen for the next.

Haley stood in the middle of the kitchen when she returned for the final tray. "Good morning," Maggie said.

"Morning," Haley replied without raising her eyes. She pulled an apron off the hook and turned her back to them as she tied it around her waist. "I'm going to start in the front."

Myra and Naomi arrived a moment later. "Is Haley already here?" Myra whispered as soon as she walked in.

"She's out front," Ruby said quietly.

"Has she said anything about Vicky?" Myra asked.

"Not a thing," Maggie said. "She only said hello and that she was going to the front."

"I don't think we need to bother her about her cousin," Ruby said. "She has no doubt already been through a bunch of questions from the sheriff's department."

"So, you're not going to ask her anything about what she knows about Vicky or where your money is?" Myra asked. She stood in front of the sink with her arms folded.

"No, I'm not," Maggie said. "I don't want to ask her a thing about it. She's just a kid, and she isn't responsible for Vicky or her actions."

Myra shook her head. "I'm fully aware of that, and I'm not in any way suggesting that she is. I just wanted to know if you were going to ask her anything about it. I won't pursue her, either. I agree that this is not on her."

"I won't pretend that I am optimistic about the money Vicky appears to have stolen," Maggie said. "I'm bugged beyond words about it, but the truth is, a woman was found dead in Vicky's house, and I think that outweighs anything I'm going through."

"I think we have another concern to deal with today as well," Ruby said. "Before Haley returns, I want to discuss this with the three of you." She glanced at the swinging kitchen door before she continued. "I got an email from the head of the cleaning crew that was here yesterday. I asked him to do a little extra work for me when the clean-up was over with."

"What sort of extra?" Maggie asked. It was the first she had heard anything about it.

"I just asked him to add clean oil back to the fryer

for us," Ruby said. "That way, if there was going to be an issue with the oil leaking out again, he could catch it right away instead of the oil leaking out again all over the floor overnight."

"Okay…" Naomi said, looking unsure. "Did something happen?"

"The oil began leaking as soon as he put it in, but they were smart enough to have something there to catch it," Ruby said. "He emailed to tell me that they did a little investigating into the cause of the oil leak and figured out that there was no mysterious leak somewhere. The rings and the hoses were all intact, but the clean-out lever on the bottom was pushed all the way over into the drain position."

"It was?" Maggie asked. "Is he sure?"

Ruby nodded. "Very sure. He even sent a couple of pictures they snapped of the position of the lever. No wonder the oil drained out so fast."

"What does that mean?" Myra asked. "In the years I've worked here, I have never once pushed the lever all the way over. It only has to go about halfway for the oil to start draining whenever we add new oil."

"I've been here a shorter time than any of you, and even I knew that," Naomi said. "What do you think it means?"

Ruby sighed. They could hear the clink of coffee

cups on the other side of the kitchen door where Haley was working behind the counter. "I am afraid that it looks like the lever might have been left open on purpose," she said.

"But why?" Maggie asked.

Ruby shook her head. "That part, I don't know. Maybe it was simply overlooked, but I think we need to ask Haley about it."

Maggie groaned, knowing she was going to have to be a part of that conversation. She didn't want to believe that her new employee would do something like that on purpose, but it was something she was going to have to face.

CHAPTER EIGHT

"I don't know why you're asking me about this," Haley said just after the first rush of customers had left the shop.

Maggie gestured for Haley and Ruby to join her at the far booth where she liked to take her break. It was mostly out of earshot, and with Myra handling the front, she knew they'd be able to talk.

"I'm asking you because you were the last one tasked with draining out the old oil and replacing it," Ruby said as she sat down.

"That doesn't mean that I did it on purpose," Haley leaned back in her seat and narrowed her eyes as she spoke.

Ruby shook her head. "I never said that I suspected you did it on purpose, but it was an expensive mistake, and it's sort of a requirement that we sit down and talk about things when something like this happens."

"So, you're blaming me?" Haley said.

"I'm only saying that the rest of the crew didn't touch the fryer, but you did. For that reason, it's reasonable for me to talk to you about it. It's also reasonable to think that you probably left the lever turned toward the drain side by accident, which led to the issue."

"Okay, so why didn't it all drain out right away?"

"Because there is a reserve under the fryer that collects some oil," Ruby explained. "Since you were the last one in the kitchen, it makes sense it could have happened that way. If you remember correctly, you were closing up in the back that day and Josie was out front. If you both walked out the front door, it's possible you didn't notice it."

"So, this is her fault then," Haley challenged. "She's been here longer and should have been paying attention."

"This is no one's fault," Maggie said, starting to lose patience. "We're just trying to figure out what happened."

Haley sat at the table with her head bowed and her

hands folded. "I should have stayed home from work today."

"Why would you stay home from work?" Ruby asked gently.

"Because I know what's going on around here."

"What is it that you think is going on around here?" Maggie asked.

"Look, I might be young but I'm not an idiot. I know my cousin is gone and that Maggie paid her a lot of money to handle the wedding. I know because her boyfriend sent one of his officers over to my house to question me last night."

"Haley," Ruby said. "You don't really think Sheriff Mission sent someone over to your house to question you because your cousin took off with Maggie's money, do you?"

She didn't answer. Instead, Haley folded her arms and shrugged her shoulders. She raised her eyebrows and stared at Ruby expectantly.

"Brett didn't send a deputy to your house to question you because of the wedding," she said quietly. She glanced around the dining room. Most of the tables were empty. Orson and his friend Delbert were seated at the Old Timer's table.

"Yeah? Then why did they come knocking on my door?" Haley asked.

It was then that Maggie realized that Haley somehow didn't know about the dead woman found in Vicky's house. "I went looking for your cousin, and there was a woman lying dead in her empty rental house. They aren't wanting to find her because of the money she took off with, but because the owner of the new bakery in Hunter Springs was found dead in her house."

Haley stared at her. Her eyes widened. "Wait. What? Why didn't anyone tell me yet? Why wasn't it on the news? Are you sure it wasn't Vicky?"

She nodded and reached her hand out toward the young girl. "It wasn't Vicky. I saw her myself."

"But you want me to tell you where Vicky is, I suppose," Haley said, pulling her hand away from Maggie's.

"Sure. I would love to know where Vicky and my money ran off to," Maggie said with a slight chuckle. "But I'm not going to question you over that. I wrote Vicky the check with the money I had for the wedding, not you. Nobody forced me to do it, and I won't demand any answers from you because I have faith that you would give me those answers if you had them."

Haley said nothing but managed to raise her eyes

to look at Maggie for the first time. "So, I'm not fired?"

Maggie looked at Ruby. "We aren't going to fire you for something your relative did," she said.

"What about the fryer?" Haley asked.

"Did you deliberately open the lever and let it drain out all over the donut shop?" Ruby asked.

"No, of course not," Haley said. She sat back in her seat.

"Then there would be no reason for you to lose your job." Maggie stood up from the table and headed back to the kitchen. Her heart raced in her chest. She retreated to the cooler and shut the door behind her. The conversation with Haley took more of a toll on her than she had anticipated. She felt awful that she was the one who had to tell Haley what had happened and hoped that Brett wouldn't be upset that she did. After all, maybe there was a reason no one had told her quite yet.

It was more than just the talk with Haley, that was getting to her, though. It was the exhaustion building up from weeks of small challenges, and then the discovery she made the day before at Vicky's rental house. It was also the torment in her own soul between the angst and regret she felt surrounding her wedding and the fact that a woman was dead. She hated herself for caring about the money in the middle of a murder investigation.

Naomi opened the cooler door a smidge. "Maggie? Are you alright?"

"I'm fine." She wiped the tears that had sprung in her eyes. "You can come in."

Naomi opened the door the rest of the way. "What are you doing in here?"

"Just taking a minute," Maggie said with a forced smile.

"I know you have a lot going on right now." Naomi stepped inside the cooler and shut the door behind her.

"Really," Maggie assured her. "I'm okay."

"I've been thinking it all through. We can take care of the wedding all by ourselves. Ruby, Myra, Flo, and I can cook for you. I am sure that Bradley's guys in Hunter Springs will help out, and you already have the venue. We can probably figure out the cake ourselves as well. It won't be the perfect wedding you pictured, but it will be a good one. I promise you it will be a good day."

Maggie tried to smile, but her face burned, and she could feel the heat rising in her chest and neck. "I need to get out of here," she said.

"What's the matter?" Naomi asked. She stepped in front of Maggie.

"Please, the door," Maggie said. "I need some air."

"Just slow down," Naomi said.

"I need to get out of here," Maggie said, raising her voice slightly.

"Hey, hey," Ruby said as she opened the cooler door. "What's going on in here?"

"I don't know," Naomi said. "I was just telling Maggie that we could put on a wedding for her, and I think she started feeling a little claustrophobic."

"Okay, then," Ruby said. She guided Maggie out of the cooler and led her to the office where she sat her down behind the desk. "You need to get out of here. This is too much for you."

"No." Maggie shook her head. "Naomi meant no harm. She was just trying to help out."

"I know she was," Ruby said. "That's not why you need to get out of here, though. You don't do well when things start spiraling out of your control. You're at the end of your rope with everything going on around you. I think you need to get away from here for a little while. Go for a drive. Clear your head and try again tomorrow."

Maggie sighed. "I think I need to get back to work and just let things go."

"Not going to happen," Ruby said. "I'm exercising my right to veto as your best friend and business partner. Go on and get out of here."

"But I was going to see about making some of those Mexican wedding cookie inspired donuts Bradley and Zeke made yesterday," Maggie said.

Ruby leaned against the door frame and smiled. "I've been thinking about that myself," she said. "Why don't we all gather over at my house this evening for a bonfire and a taste-testing, okay? I'll invite the usual suspects."

"Are you going to invite Haley?" Maggie asked.

"I don't know yet," Ruby said. "We'll see how the rest of the day goes."

Maggie nodded and stood up to remove her apron. She grabbed her bag and her phone and tossed the dirty apron in the hamper, and headed outside before anyone else spotted her. She made it to her car before Naomi burst through the back door.

"Maggie!" she said, waving her arms. Maggie rolled her driver's side window down as she approached. "I just wanted to apologize. I didn't mean to upset you." Her eyes were slightly red and swollen from crying.

"You didn't do anything wrong." Maggie reached her hand through the window and held Naomi's hand in her own. "Listen, this has nothing to do with our conversation in the cooler. I'm just running on empty at the moment. Ruby's right. I don't do well when things fall apart around me. I want control, and right now, I just don't have it."

"Are you sure? I know we aren't close like you are with Myra and Ruby," Naomi began.

"What are you talking about?" Maggie interrupted. "You are just as much a part of this little family as anyone else. I don't ever want to hear you say otherwise."

Naomi blinked back her tears. "Thank you for saying that. Okay, well, you go on and take care of yourself. I'm going to head back inside and take care of business."

"Deal," Maggie said. She patted Naomi's hand and released it.

CHAPTER NINE

A light rain began to fall as Maggie drove down the highway toward the lake. She had no clear destination in mind but drove as her mind reeled. The events from the past few days threatened to overwhelm her entirely. She pulled off the highway and drove around the lake, stopping her car on the other side of the public restrooms.

She watched as the raindrops fell on the surface of the lake. Tears filled her eyes as she stared at the ripples that flowed out from each drop. She watched until the tears spilled over and blinded her to the sight. For twenty minutes, she sat behind the wheel of her car, alone and sobbing, and allowed the stress to hit her head on. Her mind and her body succumbed to the exhaustion of the moment. Maggie cried until she couldn't cry another tear.

When she could see again, Maggie refocused on the lake in front of her. The rain had stopped falling. The sun was out, and the light sparkled off the small waves. She inhaled deeply and turned the key in the ignition. She pulled out of her parking spot and headed back toward the highway.

Maggie drove with purpose, although for the moment, she was unsure of her direction. After about fifteen minutes, she realized she was just a few miles from Hunter Springs. She made up her mind as she slowed down to drive through the town.

The Cake My Day Bakery was located in the middle of downtown Hunter Springs. Maggie pulled into the parking lot and parked her car. She was surprised to see the lights on and people moving around inside. She spotted a couple of people she recognized from the donut shop in town. Two of them had previously worked for her son at the Hunter Springs location, but she was not there to confront the employees who left in favor of working for the brand new bakery. She was there to ask questions.

It was standing room only when she walked inside the front door of the cheerfully decorated bakery. She smiled at the colorful array of cupcakes behind the glass of the display case. A few donut varieties were available, but the selection was basic, and the inventory was full. Based on the size of the crowd between herself and the front counter, she was sure the donuts were not the bakery's best sellers.

"Uh, can I help you?" One of her former employees approached her from the side while she was still several people back in line. Maggie glanced over at the young woman and smiled.

"I'm just here to order a cupcake," she said.

"No, you're here to check out the competition," the worker replied. Her comments had caused a bit of a stir in the crowd. Maggie glanced down at her name tag and smiled again.

"I'm only here as a customer, Riley," she said. The woman's name had escaped her at first.

"Just come with me." Riley grabbed Maggie by the arm and pulled her off to the side. Another bakery employee was seated at a small table nearby. "This is the co-owner of the donut shop." Riley dropped Maggie's arm and folded her own arms, as if she was waiting for the older woman seated at the table to jump up and attack.

"What can I do for you?" the woman said.

Maggie looked for a name tag on the woman's powder blue apron. "I'm sorry. I have no idea why this woman dragged me over here to you. I do own the Hunter Springs Donut Shop and the sister location in Dogwood Mountain, but I came in here to order a cupcake, not to start any trouble."

"You can return to work now, Riley," the woman said. She returned her gaze to Maggie. "Will you please have a seat?"

"I would really rather return to the line so I can order my cupcake and go," Maggie said.

"Sit down, Ms. Sharpe," the woman said. She waited until Maggie had pulled the chair out from the table and sat down. "Now, for starters, my name is Stacy Trent. I'm the co-owner of the bakery and I know you're probably here because you're concerned about the people who have come to work for me from your son's donut shop. Or maybe you're here to check out the competition, I'm not sure. Either way, you need to think twice before you start any trouble."

Maggie shook her head. The audacity of the woman's words rendered her stunned for a moment. "Why on earth would you assume that I'm here to start trouble?"

Stacy sighed and looked up. "That's a sweet story, but I don't think I believe you're here about a cupcake."

"Why would you think I'd show up here to start

trouble with you?" Maggie asked, halfway disbelieving the words coming out of her own mouth. "I came here curious, yes, but I am an adult and I'm not going to throw a fit at your place of business."

"Curious because you fear the impact my bakery is going to have on your donut shop?" Stacy said with a sneer.

"I find it interesting that you think your bakery is going to have that serious of an impact on my donut shop." Maggie chuckled. She started to feel like the subject of a hidden camera comedy show.

Stacy laughed at her. "You have to be kidding me," she said. "I serve donuts as well as you do. As you can see from the lobby, I'm not struggling for business."

"True," Maggie said, nodding her head. "I can definitely see that your bakery is off to a booming start but take a look at your donut display. You have a full case with a crowd this large. I have no doubt that your bakery is going very well, but my donut shop is not threatened by your small display here. There is no reason we can't coexist."

"I suppose we'll see when your donut shop is put out of business in less than a year," Stacy said with a smirk.

"Okay, well, I suppose this was a waste of time,"

Maggie said. She started to rise up in her chair. "You know, I came here curious about your wedding cakes as well, but now I think I'll pass."

"And there it is," Stacy said. "I know you're the one who found Kathleen's body, Ms. Sharpe. What I don't know is why you would show up here nosing around."

Maggie sat back down in her seat. "You knew I was the one who found the body of your business partner?"

"I did, and I can only imagine it's the reason you came here looking for something salacious or whatever."

"Salacious? What on earth are you talking about?" Maggie gasped. She inhaled slowly and forced herself to think. Something was profoundly off with the woman seated across the table from her. "If you know about me, then you surely know that the body of your business partner was found in the rental home of Vicky Byrd. What you probably don't know is that Vicky was recommended to me by an employee of mine for her wedding planning services."

"I know who Vicky is," Stacy said. "Although, I wasn't aware of the minute details of your life."

"Well, what you also wouldn't know is the fact that the same Vicky not only left town, but she left town with all of the money I had paid her in advance to plan my wedding. I'm supposed to walk down the aisle in three weeks. Three weeks. Your bakery was a curiosity to me. Part of that curiosity had a lot to do with the fact that thanks to Vicky, I no longer have a wedding cake for my wedding. I thought about asking you, but I don't think I want to order a cake from this place." She stood up at last and turned away from the table.

"Sorry if I don't buy that load of bull for one minute," Stacy called after her. "You aren't here for a wedding cake."

Maggie stopped and turned back to her. "You know, I'm sorry, too. I'm sorry for the loss of your business partner," she said. "Although I do find it ironic that I appear to be the only one in this entire place that seems to feel that way."

She turned her back to the woman and walked quickly out of the door. Her heart now pounded harder in her chest than it had when she first arrived. She got into her car and left the parking lot, headed for the neighborhood where Vicky's rental house was located. She had no real reason for going by the house, but pointed her car in that direction, anyway.

CHAPTER TEN

"You are the last person I expected to see over here," Brett said to her when she pulled to a stop across the street from Vicky's. His truck was parked in the driveway behind two Hunter Springs Police Department squad cars. Maggie stared past Brett at the small home.

"Ruby made me leave work," she admitted and glanced up at him. "I had sort of a breakdown."

"Yeah, I know," Brett said. He rested his arms on her window and bent down next to her car. "Ruby called me, but she didn't know where you went. I thought about calling you, but I decided to just leave you alone for a little while. I figured you were probably really mad at me."

"You think this is because I'm mad at you? You're

wrong," she said. "I just felt a little bit overwhelmed by everything going on around me all at once."

"Not to mention the stress of finding a body," Brett said. "So, you really aren't mad at me? When you started talking about postponing the wedding, I thought maybe you were having second thoughts about getting married. Or at least about marrying me."

Maggie shook her head. "As you know, there's been a lot of stuff going on lately," she said. "I think I've hit a wall, but not once have I questioned marrying you, Brett. The only thing I've questioned even close to that is the timing of the wedding after Vicky took off with our wedding funds."

"I needed to hear that." Brett sighed in relief. "Are you doing okay now?"

Maggie nodded her head slowly. "I think so. I stopped by the new bakery here in town."

"You did?"

"I wasn't planning to, but yes," she said. "Just to see what I could see, I guess. I was a little shocked to see that the place was open at all."

"You're not the only one," Brett said. "I was more than a little surprised by that. You would think that if your business partner was found dead, the place would shut down for a few days out of respect, if nothing else."

"That's what I was thinking," Maggie said. "And after meeting the owner, I'm even more convinced of that."

"You met her?" Brett asked. "You actually went inside and asked for the owner?"

"No, not at all," Maggie said. "I just went in there to get a cupcake. I was curious, especially when I saw that the place was open. I was vaguely curious about their wedding cakes, too."

"And the owner just happened to know who you were?"

"She didn't, but a woman who worked for Bradley did. She pulled me out of line by my arm and dragged me over to meet the lady."

"Seriously? She dragged you over to her?" Brett asked.

"By my arm," Maggie said. "Her name was Riley and she just assumed that I was there to start something. The owner, Stacy, assumed the same. She came right out and accused me of being there to look for something salacious. She knew I was the person who found the body here."

"That's interesting," Brett said. "We haven't really

released too much about it yet. How did she seem to you?"

"Blunt," Maggie said, understanding why Haley might not have known about the death yet. "She was cold and calculating."

"Wow," Brett said. "Those are some very specific words. Why do you say that?"

"Cold because there wasn't even a hint of concern or worry over her business partner's death, and every word she spoke to me sounded more like a movie script than a regular conversation," she said. "And calculating because she seemed to have a list of things she had already decided about me. Each of her responses were crafted around her assumptions. She even said that me going in there curious about wedding cakes was a 'load of bull.'"

"What else did she say?" Brett asked.

"The first thing she did was accuse me of being there to stalk the competition because I'm worried that my donut shop will close," Maggie said. "She even told me that I would be closed down in a matter of months."

"I think I might have to go back over there to talk to her myself," Brett said. "I had a deputy talk to her the first time. Now I want to speak with her myself."

"Because she was rude to me? Don't let this get personal, babe," Maggie said.

Brett shook his head and chuckled slightly. "Not that her rudeness to you doesn't matter to me, but it certainly won't sway my professional judgment. I want to talk to her because you're the second person who shared their impression of her as a cold person, especially in reference to her dead business partner."

"Do you think she is a suspect in Kathleen's murder?"

"I think she remains a person of interest," Brett said. "Speaking of suspects, I have some news about Vicky."

"You do? What news?" Maggie asked.

"We traced your check to a bank in Petunia."

"That isn't very far from here."

Brett nodded. "No, it isn't, and there's an extended stay motel about five miles from that bank."

"Are you going there to speak with her?" Maggie asked.

"I have a feeling she's at that motel, and I plan to find out. It will be a few hours before I'm able to get away, though."

"Okay," Maggie said. "I think I'm going to go for another drive. I'll meet you at Ruby's tonight, okay?"

"Where are you going?" he asked.

"Probably nowhere. I just feel like I can think better when I'm driving."

Brett eyed her carefully. "I need you to be careful. Promise me that you will be careful."

"You have my word," Maggie said. She patted Brett's hand and waited while he stood up and walked back toward the rental house and the other deputies waiting to talk things over with him.

Maggie stared at the yellow crime scene tape for an extra second, then turned her car around and headed for the highway. She drove in a general south-western direction until she reached the interstate toward the Oklahoma border.

She pulled off the highway a little while later and followed the directional signs to the small town. She was vaguely familiar with the area and drove toward the main part of town where she assumed the bank would be located along with the other businesses. She drove past a few fast food joints and turned into the parking lot of the bank.

Just why she had driven to the bank, Maggie was unsure, but she decided to search on her phone for information about nearby motels and quickly found one that advertised extended stay rates, weekly and monthly. Maggie got the address and pulled out of the bank parking lot. She drove through the small town of

Petunia, past the high school and football field, and onto a two-lane state highway.

Maggie felt a pang in her stomach as she drove. It was just after lunch, and she had skipped her normal breakfast break with Ruby at work. A few minutes later, she spotted the motel. It was located just off the highway near a truck stop and adjoining restaurant.

She decided to stop in for a quick bite. Maggie walked through the dirty glass door of the large building and wound her way through displays of candy bars and road novelties. A sign at the entrance read "please seat yourself." She made her way to a booth near the windows and picked up the menu from a rack in the middle of the table. She glanced up once and smiled at a pair of state troopers seated at a table in the middle of the dining area about twenty feet away from her table. Maggie turned her attention back to the menu. She scanned through the sandwiches and burgers as her stomach rumbled.

"What can I get you to drink?" Maggie turned her eyes to the waitress standing over her. Their eyes met and locked. Vicky Byrd was dressed in a pink and white waitress uniform. She held a glass of ice water in her hand and promptly dropped it on the floor in front of her.

"What are you doing here?" Maggie asked.

Another waitress rushed over with a mop and a handful of napkins.

"I have to go," Vicky raced to get the words out.

"No, you can't leave," the other waitress said. She shoved the mop in Vicky's hand.

Maggie picked up her phone and fired a fast text off to Brett. She set the phone down and turned back to Vicky, who was blocked from running off by the other waitress.

"She's right," Maggie said, nodding to the other waitress. "You can't leave. Unless you plan on going straight to answer the questions the sheriff's department has for you."

"Lower your voice," Vicky said. Maggie could see the stress in her eyes.

Maggie heard the chime on her phone. She glanced down at the screen. Brett had replied to her text. She quickly grabbed her phone and sent another message to give him the name of the restaurant.

"Just let me by," Vicky addressed her coworker. "I need to get away from here."

"You need to clean up your mess and take this woman's order," the waitress said.

"No, you need to be taken into custody," Maggie said. She increased the volume of her voice as she spoke.

"Seriously?" Vicky whispered. "Are you trying to get me arrested?"

"Yes," Maggie said.

"If this is about the money I took, I'll get it back to you," Vicky hissed. "I had to use it for an emergency, but I swear I'll take care of your wedding like I promised."

Maggie's efforts to be heard had paid off. Out of the corner of her eye, she saw one of the state troopers stand up. "I'm not here about the money you stole from me, Vicky Byrd," she said loudly. "I think you have some questions to answer about the body of the woman who was strangled to death and found in your deserted rental house."

Two troopers appeared behind the waitresses. One of them, a tall and broad-shouldered man with white hair, spoke first, "Did you say one of you is Vicky Byrd?"

"She is," Maggie and the other waitress said at the same time.

The older trooper glanced at the younger one and nodded. Maggie caught the name on the younger man's uniform. Trooper Kemp produced a pair of handcuffs and held them up in front of him. "Vicky Byrd, you are wanted for questioning in the murder of Kathleen Lester," he announced. He stepped around the slack-jawed waitress and turned Vicky around. He snapped the handcuffs on her wrists and led her away from the table. Maggie stood up and walked behind the troopers as they escorted Vicky through the truck stop and outside to their patrol car.

CHAPTER ELEVEN

"I can't believe it has been two weeks." Naomi sighed when she breezed past Maggie in the dining room of the donut shop. She wiped a crumb off the table in front of her then stopped and gazed out the window. "Looks like the sheriff is here." She winked at Maggie.

"I'll be in the back," Maggie announced. She headed into the kitchen and waited for him to join her. In the time since Vicky's arrest, Brett had extensively questioned her. Vicky willingly discussed the money she had taken from Maggie and, as it turned out, many others. She'd refused to discuss the murder charge without the presence of her lawyer.

It seemed as though Vicky had been scamming everyone out of money so she could get enough to start her own business. Maggie had not been in contact with her at all, and only knew what was happening from the bits and pieces Brett had shared with her.

"Are you hiding from me now?" Brett asked when he entered the kitchen.

"Of course not," Maggie said.

"Then why did you run back here when you saw me pull up?" he asked.

"I didn't see you pull up," Maggie replied. "I heard Naomi say you arrived."

"And that sent you running back here? Maggie, what is going on with us? You don't want to talk about anything. You don't want to go on with the wedding next week. You don't even want to plan another date. Be honest with me right now. Is it that you just don't want to marry me anymore?"

"No, that isn't it." Maggie turned her head away from his gaze. The hurt was evident in his eyes, and she could hardly find the words to describe her feelings to him. Until Vicky's arrest, Maggie had held out some hope that the woman would return the money for the wedding. How could she explain to Brett that everything seemed tainted and cursed now?

"Then what?" he asked. "Why can't you talk to

me about it? We've always been able to talk to each other."

Maggie nodded. "We have been," she said. "You're right about that. But something is different here."

"Nothing is different," Brett said. "It's us. You and me. Sure, there have been other situations around us that have been difficult, but we are still us."

"I know who we are," Maggie said. "Or at least, I know who you are. I'm not so sure I know myself very well at all anymore."

"I know you," Brett said. He approached her and held her hands in his. "I know who you are, and I know I want to marry you. Just say you'll do it. We'll put something together and tie the knot in front of the people who love us the most."

"Right now isn't the time." She pulled her hands away from his.

He said nothing more. He simply turned around and walked back out of the kitchen.

Maggie turned her focus back to the newest donut flavor. Ironically, it was the Mexican wedding cookie that Bradley and Zeke had made a couple of weeks before in honor of her upcoming wedding. She added almond paste to her favorite sweet roll dough and formed them into donuts. After the donuts came out of the fryer, a gooey center made with almonds and powdered sugar was added before the entire still warm donut was rolled in even more powdered sugar.

"Brett just left here looking like he lost his best friend," Ruby said when she appeared in the kitchen a few minutes later.

"I think he just did." Maggie sighed. "I think he's done. Really done." She expected the tears to start rolling down her face, but none came. She exhaled slowly and went back to rolling the donuts in sugar.

"Maggie, this is insane," Ruby said softly. "Nothing is stopping the two of you from getting married but you. I don't get it."

"I don't either, to be honest with you. It just seems like the moment has passed us by."

"Hey, Maggie," Myra interrupted. She poked her head through the swinging door. "There's a woman out here to speak with you. She says she knows you."

"Did you get a name?" Maggie asked. She wanted to tell Myra to send whoever it was packing.

"Riley Jeffries," Myra said.

"Oh, jeez. What is she doing here?" Ruby asked.

Maggie walked past Myra and headed back into the dining room to find Riley standing just inside the door.

"Can we go outside?" she asked when Maggie

approached. Maggie nodded and gestured toward the door. She held it for Riley and followed her outside.

"What can I do for you?" She was cold and aloof, remembering the younger woman's behavior toward her in the bakery.

"It's Stacy," Riley said. "I don't think she is a very good person."

"What do you mean?" Maggie asked.

"I mean, I caught her shorting my hours," Riley said. "She changed the hours I logged on the chart in her office."

Maggie shook her head. "If you came here asking me to intervene with my son to help you get your job back at the donut shop in Hunter Springs, I'm afraid I can't help you," she said.

"No, that's not it," Riley said. "I confronted her about it. Stacy picked up a knife from the sink and told me that I better shut my mouth about it. She told me if I knew what was good for me, I would just be quiet and let things go."

"Did she point the knife at you or put it up to you in any way?" Maggie asked.

"No," Riley said. "She just ran her finger up and down the blade, smiling. She was smiling when she threatened me, Maggie. I'm scared to death of her now."

"Did you quit? Are you planning to go back there?"

Riley shrugged and shook her head. "I don't know what to do. I can't quit."

"Why can't you quit?"

"Because she'll come after me," Riley said. "I can't just walk away."

"How do you know that?" Maggie asked. "What are you not telling me?"

Riley covered her head with her hands. "Because I know things," she said. "I know things about Stacy that could get me killed, next."

CHAPTER TWELVE

Maggie made an excuse about heading to Bradley's donut shop to help out. Ruby eyed her for a moment before she took off, then asked her to check in when she was done. Maggie left her best friend with more questions than she'd intended, but she didn't have the time to answer everything just then.

She called Brooks on her way out of town to inform him of the situation and to tell him that Riley was on her way to him at the Dogwood Mountain Police Department. She ended the phone call when he asked her where she was headed.

She drove straight for the town of Hunter Springs. It was late in the morning when she pulled into the Cake My Day Bakery parking lot and parked on the far side close to the dumpsters. She shoved the front door open and pulled out her phone. As she walked inside, she double-checked to make sure her location settings were on.

"What are you doing here?" Stacy demanded from the other side of the counter.

"I have a question for you," Maggie said. Her heart thumped so hard as she spoke that she could feel her pulse in her throat.

"Oh, you do, do you?" Stacy sneered. "Maybe you should just save your question and leave while you are ahead."

Maggie looked around at the lobby of the shop. The place was mostly empty, but there were a few people seated in the dining area. Stacy's blatant response shocked her. "I think you have something to tell me about your conversation with Riley Jeffries," Maggie said. She felt the adrenaline pumping in her veins. She balled up her fists and dared Stacy to say something.

"Riley spoke to you?" Stacy asked. Maggie caught a glimpse of something in her face. She wondered if it was fear. Or maybe, mere irritation.

"Yeah," Maggie said. "I spoke to Riley just a little while ago and she had a lot of interesting things to tell me about the way you do business around here."

"How I do business here is nobody's business but my own," Stacy said. "I think you need to leave."

"And I think you need to have a conversation with the sheriff's department about where you really were when your former business partner disappeared," Maggie said. She didn't lower her voice as she spoke.

This time, her words elicited a reaction from Stacy. She narrowed her eyes at Maggie and pursed her lips. "You really ought to shut up and leave right now," she said. "While you still can."

"Why is that?" Maggie questioned loudly. "Are you going to pull out a knife and threaten me, too? Or do you save that for your young employees?" She turned on her heels and headed back out of the door, hoping her message got through to the woman. She wanted her scared of what she knew.

Maggie made it to her car before she swore she felt the presence of someone behind her. She looked around and found the parking lot empty. She walked around the front of her car and opened the door, but before she could climb inside, she felt something around her neck. Immediately, her hands went up in an attempt to defend herself. Maggie felt fabric bunched up around her throat. Someone was behind her, and pulling hard on whatever it was that was around her neck.

Maggie stepped away from her car, her hands gripping the object around her throat. She tried to pry it off of her neck, but the pressure increased instead. She went to her knees and leaned forward. She could feel the weight of the person behind her shift. The pressure on her throat released and Stacy fell forward on the asphalt in front of her.

"You want to tell me what Riley told you?" Stacy hissed. She grabbed the side of the car and pulled herself back to her feet.

"She didn't tell me any more than you just confirmed," Maggie said. She took her phone out and quickly dialed Brett's number, then set the phone on the roof of her car. "You just tried to strangle me."

"If at first you don't succeed." Stacy smiled. She lunged forward at her. Maggie deflected her with a hard kick to her abdomen.

"I didn't show up at your bakery to start a fight with you," Maggie said.

"You think this is a fight? I'm not fighting with you," Stacy said. "I'm going to shut you up once and for all."

"Like you shut Kathleen Lester up?" Maggie smirked. "You wrapped something around her neck, too. Only she couldn't throw you off of your feet. Somehow you got the advantage over her, and you killed her. You wanted her dead so you could have this business all to yourself. No matter what you say now, there's proof against it. Riley was honest with me, and you are anything but."

"You can't prove that." Stacy sneered. "You showed up at my business and started something with me. I'm only defending myself here. That other woman is sitting behind bars for Kathleen's death."

"But as Riley just so kindly informed me, you weren't where you said you were when Kathleen disappeared," Maggie said. "You told the police that you were doing inventory with an employee the night before Kathleen's body was found. That employee only told the cops what you told her to. You convinced her you were innocent, and then you started threatening her. What did you think was going to happen, Stacy? Did you think cheating one of your employees out of their wages and then threatening them with a knife was going to end well for you?"

Stacy didn't say another word. She lunged for Maggie again. This time, she hit the side of the car and knocked the phone on the ground. Stacy managed to pin Maggie between the open door and the car. She turned around and pushed her weight against the car door.

Maggie screamed out in pain. She could feel the

pressure of the bottom of the car against her shins. Stacy pushed on the top of the door and Maggie's shoulders turned to the side as she tried to ease the pain. Stacy released the door for a moment, then bashed it hard against Maggie's body.

Maggie felt herself go dizzy. She fell against the car and slid down the side. Her head throbbed. She could feel the warm trickle of blood down her scalp. With both of her arms against the car, she pulled herself back up. Stacy remained on the other side of the car door. She pushed on the door and slammed it against Maggie again.

The door caught her shoulders and she felt sharp pains across her chest and her back. She stumbled slightly and fell down on the driver's seat. Her phone was still somewhere on the ground, and she hoped Brett had gotten her call.

Stacy remained outside of the car door. She sneered at Maggie and pulled the door open once more, reaching her arm inside. She gripped a handful of hair and pulled Maggie out of the car. Maggie's face banged against the car door. Her eyes filled up with tears from the impact. She couldn't see for a moment but felt herself dragged over the asphalt below her.

"Stop where you are!" Brett's voice shouted in the distance. Immediately Stacy released her grip.

Maggie rubbed her eyes and stood up to see what had happened. She turned to see Brett standing in front of the pickup truck with the sheriff's department logo on the side.

"This isn't what it looks like," Stacy insisted. "She showed up here and started making trouble for me. I'm just defending myself."

"That's not what it looked like to me," Brett said. Maggie spotted two more deputies circling around behind them. "I don't think that's what the judge is going to believe either."

"This is my property," Stacy said. "I'll just tell the judge that she showed up and threatened me."

"Well," Brett said, lowering his weapon. "That's all fine and dandy, but I don't think any of that will matter when I charge you with the murder of Kathleen Lester."

Stacy stiffened when another deputy pulled her arms backward behind her. She was swiftly secured in a pair of handcuffs and led away to a waiting car.

"Whoa," Maggie said. "Thanks for answering your phone."

Brett stared off in the distance before he turned to

look at her. "What were you thinking?" he asked. "You could have gotten yourself killed!"

"I know, but Riley stopped by the donut shop and told me that she had lied about Stacy's alibi," Maggie said. "She said that Stacy and Kathleen fought constantly, and Stacy wanted her out of the picture."

"We can't do this anymore," Brett said. "I can't deal with you running off and putting yourself in danger."

"I'm not going to change who I am," Maggie said. "You are supposed to be in love with the person I am."

"And you are supposed to be my wife in a week," Brett said. "But for some reason, you don't think you can be any longer. And now you run out here and put yourself in danger. It's a half hour drive to Hunter Springs from Dogwood Mountain. At any point you could have called me and filled me in on what was going on."

"Maybe I needed to figure things out for myself," Maggie said.

"This isn't the first time we've had this discussion," Brett said. "When we get married, you can't do this. You have to let me handle the police work."

"Maybe we aren't meant to get married," Maggie

said. "Maybe Vicky taking all of our wedding money is an omen."

Brett shook his head. "Don't do this," he said. "All I'm asking for you to do is take better care of yourself, and to communicate with me before you run into danger."

"I just don't know anymore, Brett. I don't think this is going to work."

CHAPTER THIRTEEN

Maggie woke the next morning to the sound of tapping on her bedroom window. Her eyes were swollen from the tears she had shed the night before. On the day that was supposed to be her wedding day, the last thing Maggie wanted to do was wake up early to company from anyone.

"Come on," a small voice called outside her window. "Wake up! Get up!" Maggie threw the covers back and pulled back the curtains from her bedroom window. She looked directly into the tiny face of her grandson Wyatt who was held up to the window by his father.

"Give me a second to get dressed and I'll meet you at the front door," she called through the window.

Bradley pulled Wyatt away from the window and nodded at her with a smile. Maggie rushed around her room and dressed quickly. She padded down the hall into the living room and turned the knob to release the deadbolt lock.

"What are you two doing here so early?" she asked when she opened the door.

"We have a two-fold purpose," Bradley said. "One, we wanted to check on you to make sure you're okay."

Maggie nodded her head sadly. "I'm okay," she said. "What's the second thing?"

Bradley smiled and stepped back from the door. "Come on, ladies," he turned his head and called out.

"Who are you talking to?" Maggie asked. She didn't have long to wait for the answer. Ruby, Naomi, and Myra appeared behind Bradley and Wyatt and walked toward her. Each one carried a bag or a suitcase of some type or another. Maggie had an inkling that the three of them were there to take her away on a quick girls' trip for the weekend. It was a sweet gesture, but she didn't want to travel. She wanted to sit in her bed and wallow until she felt better.

"Have fun, Mom," Bradley said with a wink.

"Bye, Mimi." Wyatt beamed as his father carried him off toward their car parked out in the road.

"Good morning," Naomi sang out.

"It's time, don't you think?" Myra said.

"Time for what?" Maggie asked. "The sun isn't even up."

"No, it isn't," Ruby chimed in. "But we have things to do before it comes up and you have somewhere to be when it does."

"Listen, girls. I know what this is," Maggie said.

"You do?" Myra's shoulders dropped. Maggie read the disappointment on her face.

"I'm sorry, you guys," she said. "As much as a weekend away sounds like a dream, I'm just not up for it."

Ruby chuckled and cleared her throat. "Well, the good news is that we aren't going away for the weekend, but you're also not going to sit around this house feeling sorry for yourself."

"She's right," Myra said. "You would never let us get away with that."

"Why are you here, then?" Maggie asked. She studied the bags in their arms. "And why are you packed for a trip?"

"These clothes aren't going away clothes," Naomi said. "But you are leaving, so let's get your shoes on."

Before Maggie could argue, she was swept out the door and into Myra's large SUV. She sat in the back next to Naomi. At first, Maggie had no idea where they were headed. She asked questions, but none of the others offered answers.

"Girls, what is going on?" Maggie said when they turned onto Ruby's gravel road at last.

"Come on inside and you'll find out." Naomi smiled.

Maggie sighed and allowed them to lead her into the house through the backdoor. As soon as she walked into the large farmhouse kitchen, she found herself even more confused. Large trays covered in clear plastic had been set on every possible spot in the kitchen.

"Are these leftover donuts?" Maggie asked.

"Nope," Ruby said with a wink to Myra and Naomi. "They're fresh."

"It's not even six in the morning," Maggie said. "How in the world are they fresh?"

"These girls stayed up half the night making them," Brooks said as he entered the kitchen.

"Brooks? You're off work today?" she asked. "Or maybe not? Why are you in your uniform?"

Her question was met with laughter. "If you don't know what's going on now, we have a lot of work to do," Myra said.

Maggie took a last glance at the covered trays in the kitchen before she was swept down the long hallway and into the spare bedroom across from Ruby's bedroom. She had slept in the room a handful of times herself, but today she was shoved into a chair while Naomi went to work on her hair. Myra knelt in front of her with a palette of makeup.

Maggie stood up from the chair with her hair and makeup looking spectacular. One at a time, each of the other women had disappeared into another part of the old farmhouse and emerged looking like they were ready for a walk down the red carpet.

"It's your turn now," Ruby announced when she returned to the spare bedroom dressed in a cerulean blue sheath dress. Myra breezed around the room in a baby blue A-line dress with a darker bolero sweater over the top. Naomi sported a navy blue pantsuit with an ivory colored silk blouse.

"What am I doing?" Maggie asked.

"For right now, you're putting that on," Ruby said. She unzipped a long garment bag revealing Maggie's wedding dress."

"How did you…" Maggie asked but stopped when she was overcome with emotion.

"Brett," Ruby said with a smile.

"What do you mean, 'Brett?'"

"She means that Brett orchestrated all of this," Myra said gently.

"He's the reason we stayed up half the night making all of our favorite specialty donuts," Naomi said.

"Is that what's in the kitchen?" Maggie asked.

Ruby nodded. "That was actually your son's idea," she said. "He picked some of your favorites, like the French toast donut, your cherry vanilla scones with vanilla cream, and apple cider donuts."

"And of course, his latest Mexican wedding cookie donuts," Myra added.

"It was his idea to replace a wedding cake," Ruby said. "We hope you're not too upset."

"Upset!" Maggie gasped. "Not at all. It's perfect. I just don't know why I didn't think of it first."

"Get dressed," Myra urged. "We've got two cops in their dress blues and a cranky officiant pulling at his cufflinks."

"Officiant? Who did you find at the last minute?" Maggie asked. "And are you even sure we should do this? Does Brett really still want to marry me after everything that happened?"

"Just get dressed as fast as you can, and you'll see

all of that for yourself." Ruby ushered the other women out of the bedroom. Maggie sighed and looked at the contents of the garment bag. The familiar satin and lace brought a smile to her face. She felt the tears threatening to overcome her but blinked them back. There was no way she was going to ruin her makeup now.

"I need help with the zipper," she announced when she opened the door.

Myra rushed in and helped her. While her back was turned, Naomi produced a long veil. Ruby held it over Maggie's head and gently set it in place.

Brooks appeared at the end of the hallway. "It's time."

"Right now?" Maggie barely squeaked out the words.

Ruby nodded. "Let's go get you married." With one arm hooked in Maggie's, they walked back through the house and out the back door. Maggie was shocked to see the trays of donuts had been removed from the kitchen.

"Everything is set up in the barn," Myra said. She opened the door and stepped out of the way, revealing a small group of people smiling in the early morning light. Gretchen LeClair held on to Lexi, and stood next to Albert, the handyman at the Dogwood House.

A number of uniformed officers smiled as they passed by on their way to the barn.

Maggie was surprised to see Zeke Soren holding on to Wyatt's tiny hand. When she approached, Wyatt glanced up at Zeke, then held his small hand out for her. They walked hand in hand toward the barn, surrounded by Ruby, Myra, and Naomi.

Once everyone else was inside, Zeke raced ahead of them and held the door open. Maggie was in awe when she entered the barn. The inside was illuminated by dozens of strands of soft, twinkling white lights. Orson stood at the end of the long aisle. He nodded at her and then at Brooks and Bradley. Maggie stopped when she saw Brett in his formal uniform standing between them at the end of the walkway.

"Come on, Mimi," Wyatt urged, pulling her hand toward them. Maggie glanced down at the small boy and winked, then began her walk down the aisle to join Brett.

Orson stood proudly and winked at Maggie when she made it to the end of the aisle, then cleared his throat and began his remarks. Before he called for the pair to share their vows, Brett leaned over and whispered in her ear. "I told you, didn't I?"

"Told me what?" Maggie replied.

"I told you that I was going to marry you today,"

Brett said. "And this is the first of many promises to you I will never break."

**

If you enjoyed Do's and Donuts, check out the next book in the series, Baked Betrayal, today!

AUTHOR'S NOTE

I'd love to hear your thoughts on my books, the storylines, and anything else that you'd like to comment on—reader feedback is very important to me. My contact information, along with some other helpful links, is listed on the next page. If you'd like to be on my list of "folks to contact" with updates, release and sales notifications, etc.… just shoot me an email and let me know. Thanks for reading!

Also…

… if you're looking for more great reads, Summer Prescott Books publishes several popular series by outstanding Cozy Mystery authors.

CONTACT SUMMER PRESCOTT BOOKS PUBLISHING

Blog and Book Catalog: http://summerprescottbooks.com

Email: summer.prescott.cozies@gmail.com

And…be sure to check out the Summer Prescott Cozy Mysteries fan page and Summer Prescott Books Publishing Page on Facebook – let's be friends!

To sign up for our fun and exciting newsletter, which will give you opportunities to win prizes and swag, enter contests, and be the first to know about New Releases, click here: http://summerprescottbooks.com

Printed in Great Britain
by Amazon